First German

ON HOLIDAY

Kathy Gemmell and Jenny Tyler
Illustrated by Sue Stitt
Designed by Diane Thistlethwaite

Consultant: Sandy Walker

CONTENTS

First published in 1993 by Usborne Publishing Ltd.
Usborne House, 83-85 Saffron Hill,
London EC1N 8RT, England.
Copyright © 1993 Usborne Publishing Ltd.

2 Printed in Portugal. UE

First published in America March 1994

Speaking German

This book is about the Strudel [shtroodel] family. They are going to help you learn to speak German.

Word lists

You will find a word list on every double page to tell you what the German words mean.

Hallo
hullaw

The little letters are to help you say the German words. Read them as if they were English words.

Ich bin
ikh bin
Rainer.
ryner

Einverstanden
ine fer shtanden

Nein
nine

Ja
yah

Guten Tag
gootn tahg

Word list

Guten Tag	hello
gootn tahg	
Hallo	hi
hullaw	
nein	no
nine	
ja	yes
yah	
ich bin	I am
ikh bin	
einverstanden	OK, I agree
ine fer shtanden	
du bist dran	your turn
doo bist dran	

The best way to find out how to say German words is to listen to a German person speaking. Some letters and sounds are a bit different from English. Here are some clues to help you.

When you see a "ch" in German, it is written "kh" in the little letters. Say this like the "h" in "huge". Say *ich* [ikh], which means "I". Some "ch"s are more like the "ch" in the Scottish word "loch".

Say "sch" like the "sh" sound in "show".

When you see one of these: ß, just say it like a double "s".

The "ei" in German sounds like "eye". Try saying *einverstanden* [ine fer shtanden] which means "OK".

The letter "j" in German sounds like the English "y".

Try saying out loud what each person on this page is saying.

See if you can find Josefina the mouse on each double page.

Games with word lists

You can play games with the word lists if you like. Here are some ideas.

1. Cover all the English words and see if you can say the English for each German word. Score a point for each one you can remember.

2. Time yourself and see if you can say the whole list more quickly next time.

3. Race a friend. The first one to say the English for each word scores a point. The winner is the one to score the most points.

4. Play all these games the other way around, saying the German for each English word.

Du bist dran
Look for the *du bist dran* [doo bist dran] boxes in this book. There is something for you to do in each of them. *Du bist dran* means "your turn".

Look out for the joke bubbles on some of the pages.

3

Setting off

This is the Strudel family. They are getting ready to go away to the beach for a week. Unfortunately, everyone seems to have lost something.

Can you help by answering all of their questions? *Wo ist* [vaw ist] means "where is". Use the word list to know what the other words mean.

Everything can be found somewhere in the picture. Point to each missing object and say "it's there" in German. This is *da ist er* [dah ist air] if the object has *der* before it, or *da ist sie* [dah ist zee] if the object has *die* before it. Say *da ist es* [dah ist ess] if the object has *das* before it.

Wo ist die Zeitung?

Wo ist der Korb?

Wo ist der Regenschirm, Katja?

Wo ist das Auto, Silvia?

Da ist er, Herr Strudel.

Da ist es, Oma.

Wo ist die Angelrute?

4

Word list

wo ist	vaw ist	where is
da ist er	dah ist air	he/it is there
da ist sie	dah ist zee	she/it is there
da ist es	dah ist ess	it is there
der Ball	dair bal	ball
die Zeitung	dee tsy toong	newspaper
die Angelrute	dee ang el roota	fishing rod
der Korb	dair korp	basket
der Regenschirm	dair ray gun sheerm	umbrella
das Radio	dass rah dee aw	radio
das Handtuch	dass rah dee aw	towel
das Auto	dass owtaw	car
Herr	hair	Mr.
Oma	awma	Granny

Names

Strudel	Silvia	Katja
shtroodel	zilveeva	katya

Der, die and das

Der, die and das all mean "the", but in German all naming words (nouns) are either masculine, feminine or neuter. Masculine words have der before them, feminine words have die before them and neuter words have das before them.

When there is more than one thing (plural) the word for "the" is die.

5

Joke: What's yellow and black and wears a straw hat? A bee on holiday.

On the road

The Strudels quickly get lost. They've also lost some of their luggage on the way. Can you find it for them by following their route so far? Start at their house, which is *bei den Strudels* [by dane shtroodels] in German.

Now they want to see all the places on the word list on their way to the beach. Which way should they go? They can only pass each place once.

Word list
Remember, *der, die* and *das* all mean "the".

das Häuschen das hoyss khen	cottage
der Campingplatz dair kemping pluts	campsite
die Burg dee boorg	castle
das Café dass ka fay	café
der Bahnhof dair bahn hawf	station
der See dair zay	lake
der Wald dair valt	forest
der Bauernhof dair baowan hawf	farm
das blaue Haus dass blaowa howss	blue house
der Markt dair markt	market
der Strand dair shtrunt	beach

Can you find the windmill, the field, the church and the school on the map? Point to them and say their names out loud in German.

bei den Strudels

die Schule
dee shoola

die Kirche
dee keerkha

das Café

der Wald

der Bahnhof

der See

das Häuschen

6

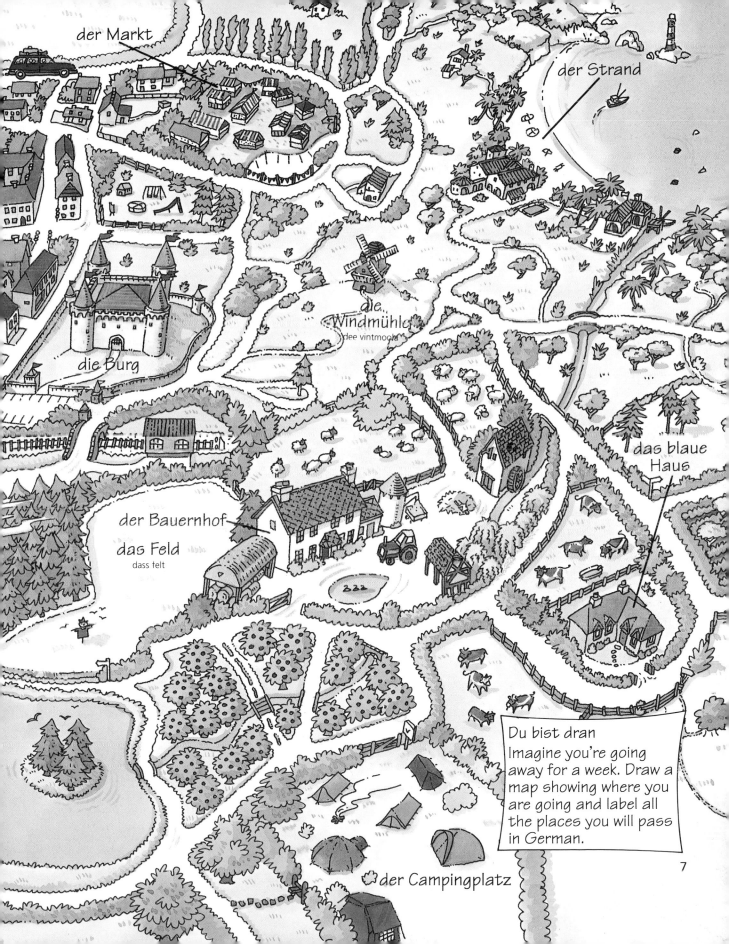

der Markt

der Strand

die Windmühle
dee vintmool

die Burg

das blaue Haus

der Bauernhof

das Feld
dass felt

Du bist dran
Imagine you're going away for a week. Draw a map showing where you are going and label all the places you will pass in German.

der Campingplatz

7

Counting game

Silvia, Markus, Katja and Uli set off to explore the countryside around the chalet where they are staying. In the forest they play a game to see who can spot the most wildlife. They write down how many of each thing they see.

Only one person has counted everything correctly. Can you see from their lists and the picture who it is?

Use the number key and word list to help you with the words.

Word list

Most naming words (nouns) change in the plural (when there is more than one) in German. *Der, die* and *das* are *die* in the plural.

die Kaninchen	rabbits	die Füchse	foxes
dee ka neen khen		dee fooksa	
eine Maus	a mouse	die Schmetterlinge	butterflies
ine a mouse		dee shmetterlinga	
die Mäuse	mice	die Bäume	trees
dee moyza		dee boyma	
eine Katze, die Katzen	a cat, cats	die Blumen	flowers
ine a katsa, dee katsn		dee bloomn	
die Hirsche	stags	ein Nest, die Nester	a nest, nests
dee heersha		ine nest, dee nester	
die Vögel	birds	wieviele	how many
dee fergl		vee feela	
die Schlangen	snakes	es gibt	there is/are
dee shlungn		ess gipt	

Number key

eins	one	sechs	six
ine ts		zex	
zwei	two	sieben	seven
tsvy		zeebn	
drei	three	acht	eight
dry		akht	
vier	four	neun	nine
feer		noyn	
fünf	five	zehn	ten
foonf		tsayn	

Names

Markus	Uli
mahrkoos	oolee

How many?

To ask "How many...are there?" in German, you say *Wieviele ... gibt es?* [vee feela gipt es]. To answer, you say *Es gibt* [ess gipt] and then the number of things. So to answer *Wieviele Katzen gibt es?* [vee feela katsn gipt ess] you would say *Es gibt zwei Katzen* [ess gipt tsvy katsn]. Can you answer the following questions in German?

Wieviele Bäume gibt es?

Wieviele Nester gibt es?

Wieviele Blumen gibt es?

Markus
sieben Vögel
acht Kaninchen
eine Maus
sechs Hirsche
vier Füchse
zwei Katzen
fünf Schmetterlinge
drei Schlangen

Katja
acht Vögel
sieben Kaninchen
zwei Mäuse
drei Hirsche
fünf Füchse
eine Katze
zehn Schmetterlinge
zwei Schlangen

Uli
acht Vögel
acht Kaninchen
eine Maus
drei Hirsche
vier Füchse
eine Katze
neun Schmetterlinge
zwei Schlangen

Silvia
acht Vögel
acht Kaninchen
drei Mäuse
vier Hirsche
vier Füchse
eine Katze
sieben Schmetterlinge
zwei Schlangen

*Joke: What's the difference between a Siberian tiger and a Bengal tiger? 10 000km. (In Germany, distance is measured in km, not miles. To change miles to km, multiply by 8 and divide by 5.)

On the beach

On the first day at the beach, the Strudel children join a beach club. To help everyone get to know each other, they have all made name and age badges to wear.

Wie alt bist du? [vee ult bist doo] means "How old are you?" Katja answers, *Ich bin sieben Jahre alt* [ikh bin zeebn yahra ult], which means "I am seven years old".

Can you say in German what Uli, Markus and Silvia are saying? What would either of the twins say? Use the number list to help you.

Number list

eins* _ine ts_	one	sechs _zex_	six
zwei _tsvy_	two	sieben _zeebn_	seven
drei _dry_	three	acht _akht_	eight
vier _feer_	four	neun _noyn_	nine
fünf _foonf_	five	zehn _tsayn_	ten

*_Eins_ only means "one" when you are counting.
"One year old" is _ein Jahr alt_ [ine yahr ult].

Word list

wie alt bist du? _vee ult bist doo_	how old are you?
ich bin...Jahre alt _ikh bin...yahra ult_	I'm...years old
wie heißt du? _vee hyste doo_	what are you called?
ich heiße _ikh hyssa_	I am called, my name is

Du bist dran

Make your own name and age badge in German. You will need: a piece of cardboard, a safety pin, sticky tape, a pen or pencil, scissors and a cup or mug.

1. Draw a circle on the piece of cardboard, using the bottom of a cup (or any round object of the size you want your badge to be) to draw a perfect circle. Then cut it out.

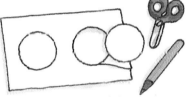

2. _Wie heißt du?_ [vee hyste doo]. Write on the circle what you are called and how old you are in German. _Ich heiße_ [ikh hyssa] means "I am called".

Look at the picture to see how to write how old you are.

Ich heiße Markus.
Ich bin 8 Jahre alt.

3. Stick a pin to the back of the circle with sticky tape. (Remember to only stick down one side of the pin so that it can still open).

11

Treasure hunt

Klaus [klowss], the leader of the beach club, has organized a treasure hunt. He has hidden the treasure in one of the red boxes in the picture.

Using the word and picture lists to help you, can you follow the clues below to find out which of the red boxes holds the treasure?

As you say each clue out loud in German, point to any of the red boxes you can see in that place. The treasure box is the only one which is in all the places on the list of clues.

Hinweise (Clues)
Auf dem Campingplatz
Hinter dem Zelt
Vor dem Baum
Neben dem Tor
Auf der Mauer
Unter dem Eimer

Word list

der Campingplatz	campsite
dair kemping pluts	
das Tor	gate
dass tawr	
der Baum	tree
dair baowm	
das Zelt	tent
dass tsellt	
die Mauer	wall
dee maower	
der Eimer	bucket
dair eyemer	

Picture list

hinter
hinter

auf
owf

unter
oonter

vor
fore

in
in

neben
naybn

Du bist dran

You could make up your own treasure hunt using German clues. Hide something and write down how to find it in German using Klaus's clues and/or any of the phrases below.

hinter dem Vorhang
hinter dame forehung

unter dem Tisch
oonter dame tish

vor dem Sofa
fore dame zawfah

unter dem Bett
oonter dame bet

auf dem Stein
owf dame shtyne

in dem Wäschekorb
in dame veshakorp

vor dem Spiegel
fore dame shpeegl

neben der Pflanze
naybn dair pfluntsa

hinter dem Papierkorb
hinter dame pupeerkorp

in dem Schrank
in dame shrunk

neben dem Fernseher
naybn dame fairn zayer

13

Guess who?

Klaus's next activity for the beach club is the Guess who? game. Everyone must pretend to be someone or something else. Klaus must guess what each child is pretending to be.

Can you see who is a mouse? Who is a king? *Ich bin* [ikh bin] means "I am". Using the word list to help you, say out loud in German what each child is thinking.

Ich bin ein Hund.

Ich bin ...

Ich bin ...

Ich bin ...

Ich bin ...

Ich bin ...

Du bist ein Mädchen.

Du bist eine Maus.

Du bist ein König.

Word list

ich bin ikh bin	I am	**ein Mädchen** ein mate khen	a girl
du bist doo bist	you are	**ein Junge** ein yoonga	a boy
ja yah	yes	**ein Mann** ine mun	a man
nein nine	no	**ein Vogel** ine fawgl	a bird
eine Katze ine a katza	a cat	**eine Königin** ine a kernig in	a queen
ein Pferd ine pfairt	a horse	**ein König** ine kernikh	a king
ein Hund ine hoont	a dog	**eine Maus** ine a mouse	a mouse
eine Frau ine a fraow	a woman		

Klaus has aready guessed what three people are. *Du bist* [doo bist] means "you are".

Can you say in German what he will say to all the others when he guesses what they are pretending to be?

Ich bin ...

Ich bin ...

Ich bin ...

Was sollte man
vass zollta mun
mit einer riesigen
mit ine a reezign
Maus nie tun?
mouse nee toon

Ich bin ...

Sich streiten.
zikh shtryten

Du bist eine Katze!

Ja, ich bin eine Katze.

Du bist dran
What are you?
You could play a Guess who? game in German with friends.

How to play:
Choose someone to be the first guesser. All the other players act out what they would like to be.

The guesser shouts out in German when he guesses someone, using *du bist* [doo bist] then what he thinks you are.

Say *ja* [yah] and then what you are in German if he is right. (Remember, *ich bin* means "I am"). You are then the next guesser.

Say *nein* [nine] if he is wrong and continue until someone is guessed correctly.

Once you have been a guesser, you must think of something else to be (or everyone will know at once what you are).

15

Joke: What must you never do with an enormous mouse? Argue.

Weather

Nobody in the Strudel family can agree about where to go on a rainy day. So Uli has stayed at the chalet with Karin and the twins while the others have all set off on different daytrips.

Which of the Strudels are joking when they phone Karin to tell her what the weather is like where they are? Use the word list to find out.

Can you say out loud in German what those who are joking should be saying to Karin?

Word list

wie ist das Wetter? vee ist dass vetter	what's the weather like?
es ist schön ess ist shern	it's fine
es regnet ess raygnet	it's raining
es ist kalt ess ist kullt	it's cold
es ist sehr warm ess ist zair vahrm	it's hot
es ist windig ess ist vindikh	it's windy
es schneit ess shnite	it's snowing
hier here	here

Names

Karin   **Helga**
kahrin   hellga

Du bist dran

Wie ist das Wetter? [vee ist dass vetter]. What's the weather like where you are at the moment? Can you say it in German?

You could write a postcard in German telling someone what the weather is like. Use the word lists, the pictures and the postcard Silvia has written to her friend, Helga, to see how to say all the words you need.

If you are writing to a boy or man you write *lieber*.

This means "How are you?"

This means "love from". German people often write this at the end of a card or letter.

Word list

lieber/liebe leeber,leeba	dear..
wie geht's? vee gates	how are you?
sehr zair	very
viele Grüße feela grewssa	love from

17

Silvia's body game

When everyone returns to the house, the rain is still pouring down. Silvia has made up a game for everyone to play.

Why don't you make Silvia's body game and play it too?

You will need: a dice, paper, pencils or felt tip pens.

Du bist dran.

der Körper

This is the shape you start with.

Word list

du bist dran — your turn
doo bist dran
ich habe gewonnen — I've won
ikh hahba gavonnen

⚀	ein Fuß
⚁	eine Hand
⚂	ein Arm
⚃	ein Bein
⚄	der Kopf
⚅	der Körper

The idea of the game is to be the first to complete a drawing of a person. Take turns throwing the dice. You must throw a 6 and shout out *der Körper* [dair kerper] to start. You can then draw the body.

Use the key above to see which numbers you must throw to add the other parts.

Say the name of each body part in German as you draw it. If you already have the part for any number you throw, pass the dice to the next player. (Remember that you need 2 arms, legs, feet and hands.)

You cannot add hands and feet before the arms and legs.

The first player to complete their person shouts out *der Mensch* [dair mensh], and is the winner. *Ich habe gewonnen* [ikh hahba gavonnen] means "I've won".

Der Mensch! Ich habe gewonnen.

Picture list

der Mensch
dair mensh
person

der Kopf
dair kopf
head

die Hand
dee hunt
hand

der Arm
dair arm
arm

der Körper
dair kerper
body

das Bein
dass bine
leg

der Fuß
dair fooss
foot

Making faces

You can play the same game with faces. Cut out lots of eyes, eyebrows, noses, ears and mouths from old magazines. Stick these on paper plates to make up your faces.

You will need:
paper plates, old magazines, scissors, glue and felt tip pens.

Play in the same way as the body game. You must throw a 6 and shout out *die Haare* [dee hahra] to start. Draw on the hair with felt tips.

Check the number on the dice against the key below to see which parts you can then stick on. Remember to say the name of each part in German as you stick it on.

die Haare

The first one to complete their head with hair, 2 eyes, 2 eyebrows, 2 ears, a nose and a mouth shouts *der Kopf* [dair kopf], which means "the head", and is the winner.

· der Mund
·· die Nase
··· eine Augenbraue
···· ein Ohr
····· ein Auge
······ die Haare

Der Kopf! Ich habe gewonnen.

Song

Here is a song about faces and bodies to sing in German. Point to each part of the body as you sing about it. You can find the tune on page 32.

Kopf und Schultern, Knie und Zehe, Knie und Zehe,
kopf oont shooltern k neeya oont tsaya k neeya oont tsaya
Kopf und Schultern, Knie und Zehe, Knie und Zehe,
kopf oont shooltern k neeya oont tsaya k neeya oont tsaya
Augen, Nase, Ohren und Mund,
owgn nahza aw ren oont moont
Kopf und Schultern, Knie und Zehe, Knie und Zehe.
kopf oont shooltern k neeya oont tsaya k neeya oont tsaya

Head and shoulders, knees and toes, knees and toes,
Head and shoulders, knees and toes, knees and toes,
Eyes, nose, ears and mouth,
Head and shoulders, knees and toes, knees and toes.

Car game

The next day dawns bright and sunny and the Strudels pile into the car to go to the fair along the coast. It is a long drive so they play a guessing game to pass the time.

The game is to give clues to somewhere and everyone has to guess where this place is.

Es gibt [ess gipt] means "there is" or "there are".

Frau Strudel starts. She says that at the place she is thinking of *Es gibt das Meer, Sand, Steine* [ess gipt das mair zunt shtyna]. This means "there is the sea, sand, rocks...". Markus guesses *Es ist der Strand* [ess ist dair shtrunt] which means "it's the beach". He is right so now it is his turn.

Use the word list to help you see what the others are thinking of. Say the clues out loud, then shout out the right answer from the answer list.

Names

Frau Strudel   Mrs. Strudel
fraow shtroodel

Du bist dran
You can play this game too. Just say *es gibt* [ess gipt] and a few of the words on the word list to describe the place you are thinking about and wait until someone guesses correctly - in German of course.

Word list

es gibt *ess gipt*	there is, there are	die Blumen *dee bloomn*	flowers
es ist *ess ist*	it is	die Pralinen *dee prah leenen*	chocolates
das Meer *dass mair*	sea	die Matrosen *dee matrawzen*	sailors
das Geld *dass gelt*	money	die Schaukeln *dee shaowkeln*	swings
der Sand *dair zunt*	sand	die Vögel *dee fergl*	birds
die Theke *dee tayka*	(shop, store) counter	die Steine *dee shtyna*	rocks
die Bänke *dee benka*	benches	die Straßen *dee shtrahssen*	streets
die Boote *dee bawta*	boats	die Autos *dee owtaws*	car
die Gebäude *dee geboyda*	buildings	die Bäume *dee boyma*	trees

Remember that in German, naming words (nouns) usually change when they mean more than one of something (plural). Most words on this list are plurals. You can see how to say the words for one of each thing (singular) on pages 30 and 31.

Answer list

das Geschäft *dass gesheft*	shop, store
der Wald *dair valt*	forest
der Strand *dair shtrunt*	beach
die Stadt *dee shtut*	town
der Park *dair park*	park
der Hafen *dair hahfen*	port

> Es gibt Autos, Straßen, Gebäude...

> Es gibt Schaukeln, Bänke...

> Es gibt Bäume, Blumen, Vögel...

> Was ist groß, *vass ist grawss* grau und macht *graow oont mahkht* "ooooo"? *ooo*

> Ein *ine* Ele-phantom. *el lay funtawm*

21

Joke: What's big, grey and goes "ooooo"? An ele-phantom.

Funny shapes

When they reach the fair, the Strudels go into the Hall of Mirrors. The mirrors make people look very different from their normal shape and size.

Silvia's reflection is too big. Markus says, *Sie ist zu groß* [zee ist tsoo grawss], which means "she is too big".

Can you say what is wrong with each person's reflection? Use the word list to find out the words for tall, small, fat and thin.

If it is a boy or a man, say *er ist* [air ist]. If it is a girl or a woman, say *sie ist* [zee ist].

Sie ist zu groß.